SET ABLAZE

AN UNBOUNDED NOVELLA

Books by Teyla Branton

Unbounded Novels
The Change
The Cure
The Escape
The Reckoning

Unbounded Novellas
Ava's Revenge
Mortal Brother
Lethal Engagement
Set Ablaze

Under the Name Rachel Branton

Lily's House
House Without Lies
Tell Me No Lies
Your Eyes Don't Lie
Zoey's Place (Novella)
Bianca's Choice (Novella)

Noble Hearts
Royal Quest
Royal Dance

SET ABLAZE

AN UNBOUNDED NOVELLA

TEYLA BRANTON

WHITE
STAR PRESS

This is a work of fiction, and the views expressed herein are the sole responsibility of the author. Likewise, certain characters, places, and incidents are the product of the author's imagination, and any resemblance to actual persons, living or dead, or actual events or locales, is entirely coincidental.

Set Ablaze (An Unbounded Novella)

Published by White Star Press
P.O. Box 353
American Fork, Utah 84003

Printed in the United States of America
ISBN: 978-1-939203-73-1
Year of first printing: 2016

To all those who struggle with addiction of one kind or another, and whose hearts yearn for freedom and release.

CHAPTER 1

THE LITTLE PORTUGUESE TOWN OF MONTE VINHA WAS strange. I couldn't put my finger on what bothered me about it, but the feeling was in every smile directed our way, the stares that followed us down the nearly deserted streets, and even the air we breathed. Yet the quaint buildings, the rich food, the friendly people—everything appeared normal, similar to the other small towns we'd passed.

But I knew something in Monte Vinha wasn't right.

A hundred and eighty years ago, I'd been born in this country, and though I'd returned only a handful of times since after my parents' deaths, it was still my homeland. Even before London, where I'd lived most of the past century, or America, where I had spent the rest of my boyhood and early adult years with my foster father, Ritter Langton.

"It's like we've stepped into some kind of comic horror movie," my partner Kenna Murray said, the lilt in her Northern Irish accent making it sound like a question. "And they're all waiting for night to turn into psychopathic killers and chop us up into wee pieces."

"Exactly," I agreed. "And where are all the tourists? There should be more walking around. They do have a castle here."

Even though I was driving, I didn't miss the roll of Kenna's eyes. "Practically every little town here has a castle," she said. "We've passed a dozen at least." A gross exaggeration since we'd only seen four or five on our drive from the airport. "Seriously, though, it's getting late in the season for tourists."

"Not here, it isn't." Mid-September was still prime tourist season. "The sudden decline in population could be keeping them away. Rumors do travel." I glanced over my shoulder as I turned off the main street, following the directions given us at the café where we'd eaten lunch.

Monte Vinha had plunged from five thousand residents to nearly four thousand in the past five years alone. That abrupt change and the chatter our Renegade technopath had intercepted about Emporium land purchases in the area was the reason we were here. Portugal had a history of remaining untouched in our battles with the Emporium, but after a thorough reconnaissance of the town, I guessed that was about to change.

"Could just be the younger generation moving away

for better jobs in the city," Kenna suggested. "And at the same time the aging population slowly dying off."

The youth in these small cities had historically left for better opportunities, but many returned later in life to take over small businesses from their parents and grandparents as the older generations retired and passed on. "If that were the case, wouldn't there be more older people here? I don't believe I've seen anyone over sixty, have you?" I'd have to check the data we'd been given to see if the population ages matched up with similar cities.

Kenna thought for a moment before shaking her head. "No, I can't recall seeing any really old people. Maybe they had a mini flu epidemic, or some kind of disease the elderly weren't inoculated for. A few hundred dying over several years might not have set off alarms until now. Either that or the Emporium has discovered the fountain of youth and is passing it along to the town, so the old people are leaving in droves for new careers too." We shared a laugh at the implausibility of the Emporium doing anything to help mortals.

Whatever was going on here, I planned to find out exactly what the Emporium was up to—and put a stop to it. That is, unless our initial report made Greggor recall me to London. I didn't fool myself into thinking that I'd been our leader's first choice for the assignment.

Only two days ago, the Emporium had slaughtered twenty of our people during a Renegade meeting in New York City, and our London cell was down five of our strongest Unbounded, four permanently dead and one missing. No, I was by far not the first choice, at least not without more backup. My abilities were extremely useful, but things tended to explode when I was around—literally. Our leader was making the best call he could with the personnel he had left. I just happened to speak the language, and as half-Portuguese, I blended in.

Kenna, by contrast, was a brilliant operative, always near the top of Greggor's list. After two hundred years of life, her fighting skills were impressive even among Unbounded with the combat ability. She spoke as many languages as I did and could lose most of her Irish brogue when she concentrated, though her red hair and all those freckles would be a drawback here without her disguise.

"Oh, wait, remember that old guy we passed in the park?" Kenna said. "He had to be a least seventy." She gave me a grin that twisted something in my gut. "Guess that takes the fountain of youth idea off the table."

I turned our rental car down a short dirt road, which should lead to our vacation rental. I'd have preferred a bed and breakfast, but a villa meant no prying eyes as we came and went, and no neighbors to run into at mealtimes. We couldn't risk Emporium agents hearing through casual conversation that we were here.

Dust billowed up the sides of the car, mostly kept out by the closed windows. A little whitewashed villa with a tiny patch of grass in the front yard appeared in the distance.

Kenna squinted through the dust. "Look, someone's waiting for us."

She checked the mirror and adjusted her long, dark wig. I could still see her myriad freckles under her thick makeup, and every one of them fascinated me.

I pulled my mind away from those thoughts. I was so far out of her league that even thinking about her that way was a waste of time. As a combat Unbounded, she was disciplined, unforgiving of weaknesses like the one that was already making my hands start to shake. I'd have to do something about the unsteadiness sooner rather than later, but I would put it off as long as possible.

I wasn't wearing a wig, but I'd grown my hair several inches longer, and let three days of beard cover my normally clean-shaven face. For an Unbounded, that meant I looked like I hadn't shaved in three or four weeks. I could pass for a thousand different Portuguese men.

Bringing the car to a stop in front of the villa, I jumped out and made my way to the narrow cobblestone pathway leading to the porch. The stocky woman sitting on a chair came awkwardly to her feet, smoothing her dress and the apron she wore over it. Her hair was still mostly dark, but her face was wrinkled by long exposure to the sun. I guessed her age to be mid-fifties.

"*Boa tarde,*" she said with a smile, ducking her head slightly.

"Good afternoon," I repeated, slipping easily into the language of my youth. "I guess we're your tenants for the week."

"Ah, I can tell by your speech that you are Portuguese," the woman's smile grew wider, her Portuguese flavored with the accent of the Alentejo. "Welcome. I am Dona Mafalda." *Dona* meant missus, but as was often common, she'd used it with her first name and not her last. Hearing it reminded me of long sunny days and simpler times.

"My husband and I take care of this house for the owner," she continued. "There are clean linens on the beds and more in the cupboards if you need them. I brought bread, cheese, ham, and the other things you requested and put them in the refrigerator. Keys are on the table. If you need anything, please call the number by the phone."

She glanced at Kenna and added, "If your wife doesn't speak Portuguese, my daughter knows English, and she can call to tell me what you need. Her number is also by the phone."

"I speak Portuguese," Kenna said, her accent passable, but with a hint of her Irish brogue. "But thank you for your kindness."

"Good, good." Dona Mafalda said. "You live in Portugal then?"

"In Leria." I chose a significantly larger city farther north, one definitely not close to where I'd been born in nearby Évora.

"Ah, that's good. It's so nice to have young people here. Monte Vinha is so beautiful, but our youth don't see that. They always want to leave."

At first, I suspected Dona Mafalda's remark was a subtle

jab at our youthfulness—an illusion since Unbounded age only two years for every hundred we live—but there was really nothing in her tone to indicate this, and her semi-vacant smile never faltered.

The woman leaned over to scoop up a very large cloth shopping bag. "I hope you will enjoy your stay. There are two bicycles on the back deck, a soccer ball, and inflatables for the pool. Let me know if you need anything." Tipping her body forward in a partial curtsey, she stepped past us and hurried down the cobblestone path to the dirt road.

When her figure disappeared, Kenna drew one of the guns we'd picked up at the safe house in Lisbon this morning. I did the same. Opening the door to the villa, we stepped carefully inside. The entryway opened into a large sitting room, featuring an aged floral couch, two matching chairs, a long black coffee table with a stack of magazines, and an oversized TV. Kenna motioned that she'd check out the two bedrooms, so I ducked into the kitchen. The room took quaintness to a new level, every gleaming surface decorated with hand-crocheted doilies like my grandmother had once made. No sign of danger.

Kenna met me back in the sitting room and together we headed for the large cobblestone deck off the back of the villa. She checked the perimeter, while I gazed at the glittering water in the pool. The water beckoned, promising to soothe the growing ache inside me, but I knew it couldn't. There was only one thing that could stop the ache.

"Let's bring in the equipment." Kenna returned to my side, holstering her gun.

"Yeah, right." But I didn't move to join her as she started to leave. The cobblestones, the whitewash of the house, the red tiles of the roof, and even the interior setup was very like the house my parents had owned in Portugal—the house I still owned—passed down first to my parents and then to me by a great-grandfather I'd never met.

The water in the pool undulated with a light breeze. I'd been swimming in the river with my friends the day the gardener had brought the awful news that my Portuguese mother and English father were gone. Killed in a fire on their trip to Lisbon, he'd said. That was long before I'd heard of Unbounded, or learned my parents' deaths weren't accidental.

"Blaze, is everything all right?" Kenna asked.

I turned to look at her, aware that the minor shaking in my hands had now become flashes of heat. Moisture washed over my entire body. "Of course."

But everything wasn't all right. These memories made me feel more out of control. Hopefully, nothing a swig of curequick couldn't dispel, but I wasn't going to drink it now. *I can wait just a little longer.* I would end up taking it because I'd never jeopardize the mission, even if drinking the curequick meant hurting myself. It was almost like a game I played at times, a deadly serious game. One I always lost.

I strode past Kenna and added, "I'll grab the computer while you sweep for bugs."

Setting up the laptop and the projector didn't take long. Soon I was staring at a large satellite image on the white wall of the sitting room, where I had removed a painting to give us more space.

Kenna came into the room with a teapot full of water. "Is there some special place that Portuguese customarily keep the matches? I was going to make some tea, but I can't light the gas burner until I find the matches. Would you like a cuppa?"

"Sounds good."

Like all Unbounded, we didn't need to eat to survive. Our bodies were continuously absorbing bits and pieces of the world around us, but we still derived comfort from food and especially the familiar. Sometimes a juicy cheeseburger helped push back my demons.

"Here." I approached her, reaching for the pot. I could see lemon rinds already floating in the water.

"Wh—" She broke off, a smile playing on her mouth. "Oh, this I have to see."

I gave a little effort, and the pot in my hand instantly heated, the water beginning to boil violently. Oops, too much.

As a *roaster,* my Unbounded ability was to manipulate matter in one specific way—heating. The ability was remotely similar to the talent of pyros, who could set fire to anything flammable, but my manipulation extended to any matter. I could increase the temperature of an object by touch, either scorching, boiling, or melting it. Bursting objects into flame was the most obvious part of the ability, though not the most effective, thus my nickname Blaze.

A side effect was that my skin could withstand incredible heat before it began to burn. Not that I was impervious to high temperature, but I could normally work through the discomfort and pain. The ability made me valuable to the Renegade cause, but using it excessively as I'd done meant I often ended up incapacitated and in dire need of curequick, which in turn had allowed the "medicine" a chokehold grip on my life.

Still smiling, Kenna went to retrieve the teacups and a plate of ham and cheese sandwiches made from the welcome package left by the landlady.

I set the still-boiling teapot on a hot pad and returned my attention to the map on the wall. Splashes of yellow marked the areas our intel had pinpointed as possibly being connected to the Emporium. Some of the purchases dated back over ten years, but it was the recent large purchases marked in red that had flagged our attention.

"With both the red and yellow, it means they own most of the land surrounding the city," I said.

"If the yellow really belongs to the Emporium."

Sometimes I wondered if Kenna disagreed with me just for the sake of argument.

"I'm betting it does, and whatever they've been doing

here, it's been successful enough that they've decided to expand." I reached to touch the teapot again, giving it a final shot of heat because it hadn't boiled quite long enough yet.

"That's farmland, isn't it?" Kenna pointed to the red areas on the satellite image.

"According to the data, it was all vineyards and cork trees at one time. And one olive grove. But you're right. The satellite images Greggor gave us don't show trees on the new land they purchased, though there are some on the yellow areas." I paused before adding, "Cutting down cork trees? That's almost a crime. It takes three harvestings of nine years apart before the very best cork is grown. That's twenty-seven years of work and patience thrown away."

"Vineyards take time too." Kenna sat on the floral sofa, crossing her knees, her eyes still fixed on the map. "And it's difficult to cut down trees at all. So what are they growing instead that is so important? Maybe some kind of GMO?"

"Genetically modified organisms? Could be. The background I was reading on the plane says Portugal has increased their use of GM crops every year."

"I thought Europe banned the use of GMOs."

"Publicly, maybe. But most countries have them in some form or another."

Kenna gingerly tested the handle of the teapot before pouring a cup for each of us. She'd found a sack of sugar—most likely left by past vacationers—and put one spoonful in mine and two in hers. I wondered how she knew my preference, but before I could ask, she was talking again.

"Still, cutting down trees hardly seems something the Emporium would waste time on. Why not just go somewhere else? With American companies pushing for GMOs, it isn't really an agenda the Emporium needs to help along. Something else is going on. Something bad."

"Well, that's what we're here to find out." Like most Unbounded gifted in combat, she had great instincts. I would trust her even if my gut wasn't giving me the same feeling. "I already emailed Greggor a request for a population comparison with other towns to see if that brings up anything." Our technopath in London could come up with the information we needed in a fraction of the time it would take us to research it.

I gulped the hot tea and eyed the sandwiches, but my desire to eat had deserted me. I couldn't push back the need for curequick any longer without endangering my ability to function. Besides, in a minute, Kenna would see that I was suffering.

"You up for a bike ride?" I asked her. "Let's see what they have growing in their fields now."

Kenna's laugh was genuine. "Actually, I haven't ridden a bicycle in fifty years."

"Don't worry. It's like . . . like . . ."

"Riding a bike?"

I laughed. I'd spent most of the last decade largely avoiding working with a single partner. Mostly, I was sent in alone, while a team worked the same op from another angle. My goal was to complete whatever missions I was assigned until I was too damaged or too exhausted to continue, and then I'd spend weeks in my flat recovering. That meant a lot of solitary moments. It felt good to be working with a partner again.

"I'll just change into some shorts," I said. "Trifle hotter here than in London."

Grabbing my duffel, I headed to the smaller of the two bedrooms. I forced myself to wait until after I changed, my body flushed and sweating, my stomach cramping, to get the curequick from my pack. Curequick was a staple for all Unbounded regeneration, despite its addictive properties, and we usually carried it in both drinkable and injectable versions. Made primarily of sugars and proteins reduced to their most usable forms, it allowed us to regenerate at five times the rate of our already increased regeneration level. It also gave the user a pleasant buzz. The mixture had been designed by a scientist in one of our American Renegade cells, strictly formulated for use after taking wounds in combat. Unfortunately, Unbounded who used it too often found themselves victim to the severe withdrawal symptoms.

Unbounded like me.

For years, I'd told myself I was different from the new generation of Unbounded, who used curequick as a recreational drug, not as a way to heal after battle, but in the end it all boiled down to the same thing. Too many missions, too much curequick, and I was no longer reliable. The only thing left was to check myself into a certain hospital in London for treatment, and I'd be damned if I was going in that direction. No, I'd fix myself.

After this op.

It was always after the next op.

I downed the contents of a pouch, and the warmth spread through me, at first a trickle and then a rush.

I loved it—and I hated myself for needing it.

Of course, if I had been reliable and not in the habit of avoiding extended meetings because of my dependence, I would have been in New York with the others when we were betrayed to the Emporium. I might have been one of those slaughtered. Instead, I'd have to live the rest of my two thousand years—twenty-five lifetimes of guilt— knowing I hadn't been there to protect our people.

A noise at my door had me reaching for my gun, but it was only Kenna, her eyes narrowing as she spotted the pouch in my hands. "Look, if you can't do this . . . I heard about your . . . trouble."

"My addiction, you mean. It's not a problem. I'm dealing with it, okay?"

"Sure." The firm line of her jaw told me if there came a time when I wasn't handling it, she'd make sure I didn't endanger the mission.

"Anyway, right now we have a bigger problem," she continued. "I was moving the bikes out to the path behind the house, and I found something. Remember those old people we were looking for? I found another one, but he's dead."

CHAPTER 2

THE MAN'S LEATHERED FACE POINTED UPWARD, HIS EYES open and unseeing.

"You sure he's not just smashed?" I asked, kneeling to check his pulse.

"Of course I'm sure. And for the record, he doesn't even smell like alcohol."

"He can't be older than sixty." I rummaged through his pockets. "Wallet's here . . . with money."

"No obvious signs of trauma, either. Looks too young to have died of old age." Kenna glanced around. "We have to move him. Can't let the authorities come to the house or think we're connected."

"We're not connected."

"No, but if the Emporium owns all the land around the city, I bet they own the authorities. This will call attention to us."

"I'll get the gloves in my pack."

Gloves and a white bedsheet were all we needed to carry the man through the deserted grove of thin-leafed olive trees bordering the property. Tall bushes that were almost trees themselves often barred our way, telling me this particular grove wasn't cultivated. We deposited the body far enough away from the villa that we wouldn't be suspected, but close enough to a small grouping of houses that someone was bound to find him soon.

"Careful where you step," Kenna said as she folded up the sheet we'd used. We'd have to dispose of it later, not that I was expecting much from local law enforcement.

"Poor guy," Kenna added, staring down at him. "Hey, what are you doing?"

"Taking a blood sample." I inserted the needle into his calf, where the hair should go a long way toward hiding the mark. "How many other dead mortals have you discovered lying around on other missions? We both know something is going on in this town. It might be—"

"Connected," she finished. "I know—it's just that I already took a sample before we moved him." She shook her head and sighed. "It's so peaceful out here. Hard to believe the Emporium chose this place."

"They're everywhere." I purposely made my voice hard. "Let's go."

Back at the villa, Kenna tossed the sheet in the bathtub and filled it with water and bleach. Then she changed her clothes. She always did that after any kind of fight or op, as if changing wiped away the memories.

Whatever she needed to do.

"What are you staring at?" she asked, as she climbed on one of the bicycles.

I dragged my eyes from the legs that emerged quite compellingly beneath the patterned shorts with the over-sized pockets. I'd been attracted to Kenna for most of the past five years, but even if I didn't have a problem with curequick, Renegade Unbounded were careful about their relationships—and for good reason. Our genes ensured that children would invariably result from almost any union, and there was no guarantee the offspring would be Unbounded. We'd all learned too well that having a family meant watching most of them grow old and die before we'd aged two years. It meant stress-filled years of actively protecting loved-ones from Emporium slaughter. I'd seen many of our people watching over their posterity for six generations with the hope that someone in their line carried the active Unbounded gene.

No, even if Kenna was interested, a relationship wasn't something I could risk until I got myself under control. I wasn't reliable.

I flashed her a grin. "I'm not staring. I'm just hoping we aren't going to be climbing in the bushes, or we'll both be uncomfortable."

"The satellite images show paths all around this area and most of the fields. We only have to get close enough to see what's going on, and take a few samples."

Hopefully, not more blood samples.

"Let's check out the buildings last," I suggested.

There was only one set of buildings large enough to be of interest. "I bet we won't be able to get too close."

"Probably not."

The first field was only ten minutes away, but the crop had already been cut down. "Corn," I said, squatting down to examine the remaining stalks.

In the next field, cabbages were being harvested by a dozen Portuguese who loaded them into a long, wagon-like trailer pulled by a truck that showed more rust than green paint. Only one woman glanced our way as we pedaled by. We waited until they were out of sight to gather a sample and put it in my pack.

We passed fields of potatoes, carrots, and tomatoes before coming to wheat fields that went on as far as we could see. I took a sample as I had with the other fields and said, "I think we've seen enough here. Fresh daily bread is a staple in Portugal, so these probably go on for a while. I'd like to look at those vineyards and the olive grove we saw on the map. If the Emporium is behind those, they've been here for at least ten years."

"The buildings are near the vineyards too. We need to see those."

We reached the olive grove first, and the beautifully tended trees brought a lump of nostalgia to my throat. Olive oil was as common as water here, and I still used it whenever I had time to cook.

Next came the vineyards, the sweet grapes beckoning to us on the vines. I was already experiencing the faint taste of grapes through absorption, as my body sucked in nutrients from the world around us, but I couldn't resist stopping. Picking and eating grapes from the fields on the way to our swimming hole was straight out of my childhood. Hopping off the bike, I grabbed several bunches of the bulging fruit.

Kenna settled next to me on the remains of a crumbling stone wall that had once encircled the field. "Don't you think it's stupid eating these without knowing what the Emporium is doing here?" she asked as I held out a cluster to her.

I laughed. "I guess I'm too accustomed to being immune to everything. Besides, it's not Unbounded who are dying here."

"Just because severing our focus points is the only proven method for killing Unbounded doesn't mean another way isn't possible. I'm fairly certain Emporium experimentation is how we learned about the whole lock them in a sealed room for decades until the body falls apart approach." Taking a tube from a back pocket, she dropped in one of the grapes before adding a squirt of liquid from a vial stored in yet another pocket. Even Kenna's casual clothes were especially designed for combat, and I was betting she had at least ten other pockets holding different weapons and tools. I used to order similar clothing, but more often than not, they ended up burned and unusable after an op, so I'd given up on them.

Shaking the tube, she smiled. "No toxins at levels that should hurt us."

"Course not." I threw a grape at her, intending to catch her off guard.

Her hand, barely a blur, shot up to catch the fruit. "I didn't say there aren't *any* toxins. This test isn't that sensitive." She popped the grape into her mouth. "Mmm," she said with an exaggerated sigh. "Whatever they're doing here, they haven't compromised on taste like most of the genetically modified foods in the world today." She shook her head. "I don't even bother with strawberries anymore unless they're straight from my own garden."

"You have a garden?"

She shrugged. "I dabble. Just a few years now."

Right. And I'd been trying to stay away from her for at least that long. "It doesn't make sense, all these different foods. I mean, there is no sign they're exporting or even selling outside the region. They might own the land around the town, but in the scheme of things, it's only a tiny bit of land. Really not more than enough food to feed this town and maybe a few more. They can't be making money."

"We need Drew." Kenna's voice caught on the words, but her expression was even.

Drew Gunnel was one of those we'd lost in the New York raid. I knew he and Kenna had been close, but I didn't know how close. He'd also been a scientist who could do wonders in the lab. Normally, he would have come along on this op; now we'd have to send our samples to his mortal assistant in London.

"We'll figure it out," I said. "But I think our answer is over there." I jerked my head in the direction where my GPS had pinpointed the buildings.

Kenna nodded and brought up on her phone the notes we'd made earlier. "According to the records Greggor pulled, the original main building was built at the same time this vineyard was purchased ten years ago. But in the past two years, they've doubled its size and added a bunch of what might be large storage barns."

I swallowed the rest of my grapes. "Let's go see." The sun was low in the sky, but there were still several hours left of daylight.

"Be careful. They'll have cameras."

When I didn't respond, she added, "Sorry, force of habit."

Combat Unbounded liked running the show, which was often annoying for the rest of us who trained just as hard and knew the rules. "I don't mind. I'll be careful."

Her smile sent heat curling through my belly, a burning sensation that had nothing to do with my ability and everything to do with how much I liked being with her. I hadn't been in a relationship to speak of in fifty years, and I would be blind not to be attracted to Kenna.

Leaving the bicycles, we wound our way through the vineyard, careful to keep the vines between us and the buildings that rose in the distance. Finally, there was only one row of grapevines left to shield us, and we squatted down to peer around them with our binoculars. The place was surrounded by a chain-link fence topped by razor wire. If that wasn't a big enough clue, the uniformed guards standing at the gate and intermittently around the fence were a clear indication that this wasn't your average agricultural company.

I counted at least eight newer buildings, made from corrugated metal or wood instead of the brick and cement typical to the region—probably hastily constructed. There were also two crumbling brick buildings, and nearest the main gate, an older, squat edifice with fresh mustard stucco. Guards came and went from the yellow building, some strutting with an overt confidence that hinted at an Unbounded nature.

"Well, look at that," I said as the workers we'd seen earlier picking cabbages drove up with their wooden wagon full of produce. The guards let them through the gate, and I followed the wagon with the binoculars until it reached a wooden barn-like structure behind the main yellow building. The double doors opened wide to reveal stacks of crates.

Before the workers finished sorting their cabbages into the crates, four other groups arrived with what had to be more produce. The workers looked happy and smiled as they waved to the guards. One of the female employees jumped down from a truck and ran toward a guard, who swept her up in his arms and kissed her, his hands eagerly groping her body. The other guards poked each other playfully and pointed at their comrade, goading him on.

I wasn't surprised. The Emporium always left a slew of abandoned women and illegitimate babies in their wake. Babies they'd only send someone to check on after thirty years, in case they carried the active Unbounded gene and Changed.

"The workers don't seem afraid." Kenna put down her binoculars, fitting them into a zippered side pocket in her shorts.

"The Portuguese are hard workers, and the economy here isn't great. I bet they're glad to have jobs." I hadn't seen any old people in the mix of workers, though I didn't point it out. The Emporium would naturally employ people they thought could endure hard work.

"Obviously, they're not planning on making this a real business," I said, returning to our earlier conversation. "Or they would have brought in more machines and purchased even more land. There's not even enough wheat to supply more than the city with flour. Whatever they're doing is localized."

"Testing, then."

"That's my bet." I suddenly became aware of how close we were sitting. My mouth felt dry as my gaze locked onto her face. Much of the makeup she'd worn was gone, and a trickle of sweat sliding from under her wig hinted at the reason. Usually we dyed our hair every other day during ops, to account for rapid hair growth, but we'd expected this to be more of a reconnaissance than a combat operation.

With the dead man outside the villa, all that had changed. Meaning the op was working up to be pretty average fare for Renegades. Most of our ops had casualties, though we tried to make them happen on the side of the Emporium and not the innocent mortals we protected.

"I'll text the courier to meet us at the villa," Kenna said, drawing out her phone. The courier service we'd contacted this morning in Lisbon employed a driver in a nearby town who would come for the samples and fly them back to London. The exorbitant price tag on the remote pickup was more than worth getting the samples there before noon tomorrow, and they had promised to send the courier in civilian clothing so as to not attract attention.

We zigzagged across the field, keeping low until the buildings dropped out of site on the horizon. At the bikes, I dug into my pack and took out the samples I'd gathered from the other fields. "Why don't you take these and meet the courier at the villa? No sense in both of us waiting around. I'll go into town and see what I can learn about the man we found."

She opened her mouth to protest, and I wondered if Greggor had warned her to keep me in sight.

"I'll be fine," I said before she could speak. I had plenty of curequick in my pack, if I needed it. Being a native, I was the obvious person to snoop around, and getting the samples to the courier was vital, which meant it was Kenna's responsibility.

"I was just going to say we have company." She looked past me as she spoke, shifting her body into a defensive stance.

I adjusted my position casually, catching sight of two men coming toward us. The heat built inside me as I prepared for a fight.

CHAPTER 3

THEY WEREN'T DRESSED LIKE EMPORIUM AGENTS, AND THEY looked Portuguese, though that didn't say much. The Emporium had many mortal employees. These men didn't look any different from the field hands we'd seen earlier.

Workers, I guessed, *going home for the day.* I didn't relax my readiness, though. The Emporium could be using them.

"*Boa tarde,*" they murmured, nodding.

"Good afternoon," I echoed in Portuguese.

One of the men hesitated, but when his companion didn't pause, he hurried on without stopping. We watched them disappear down the narrow dirt road.

"That's weird," I said. "Portuguese in the country *always* stop to chat. They want to know everything about you."

Kenna laughed. "Ah, give 'em a break. They look knackered. Probably worked all day."

"That's just it, they should be excited about going to a pub or something, but they're heading away from town."

"Maybe they need to go home and shower."

"I guess." The path leading back to the villa was in the same direction the men had taken, and now it was me who was reluctant to let Kenna go, though she could best me in a fair fight. Those two didn't look like Emporium agents, and twenty just like them wouldn't be a match for her.

"I'll see you later then. Stay out of trouble." Climbing onto her bicycle, she rode off without waiting for a response.

I headed in the other direction. It was only ten more minutes before I reached the edge of town. The few people out and about stared at me as I passed, smiling and nodding. The stares weren't unusual. In the larger cities, you almost never saw a Portuguese riding a bicycle—the traffic on the roads and the crush of humanity on the sidewalks made it too difficult. While bike riding was more common in smaller towns, walking was still the preferred mode of transportation for all but the very young. Clearly, I'd been pegged for a tourist. Not exactly the best way to blend in, but there was no changing that now.

I'd ridden up and down almost every street in the town, finding nothing unusual besides the stares, before I steered toward the hospital. An ambulance was pulled up there, and I recognized Dona Mafalda standing near it with a vacant smile on her face.

Leaving the bike, I went to her side. "Hello again."

She turned toward me as if trying to remember who I was.

"I'm staying at the villa? Just came in a few hours ago."

"Oh, yes. Are you enjoying your stay? Do you need something?" Her gaze pulled toward the hospital door, and then back to me.

"No, we're getting along fine. Is everything okay?"

"Yes. It's a beautiful day, isn't it?"

"Someone's not sick I hope," I said.

A fleeting frown and another glance toward the hospital. "No, not sick."

I was about to press further, when a little, bubble-shaped orange car screeched up to the curb and a woman in her mid-thirties jumped out. She was thin, though tall for a Portuguese woman, and mad as hell.

My hand moved toward the gun tucked in a holster at my back, the bulge hidden beneath my T-shirt, but the woman didn't glance at me as she rushed to Dona Mafalda.

She threw her arms around the older woman. "He's dead? Really dead? I told you something would happen, that you needed to leave this town. It's a death trap. Why didn't you listen?"

Dona Mafalda enfolded the newcomer in her embrace. "Everything is fine, daughter," she said, using the term daughter like an endearment. "Everything is fine."

The younger woman pushed away. "It's *not* fine. Papa's dead. DEAD! And you call me like he just has a cold."

"Bridida, calm yourself. It was his time, that's all, my love."

"No it wasn't! Mother, can't you see? Something's wrong here. I'm worried about you."

"Me? But I'm perfectly fine." Dona Mafalda's brow wrinkled with confusion.

"You're not fine. And you're coming home with me. I'm getting you out of here. Something's in the water or the air. Papa's gone, and I'm not losing you too."

"But my café, and the villa . . . new guests arrived today." Dona Mafalda's gaze moved in my direction, as if asking for help.

Her daughter whirled around to glare at me. "Who are you?"

I made my voice as mild as possible. "Paulo. I'm staying at the villa. Your mother takes care of the place."

"Not anymore. I'm sorry. Just leave the key under the mat when you leave. I'll tell the owner." The anger in Brigida's eyes pierced me. "But I wouldn't stay here if I were you."

This brought Dona Mafalda out of her daze. "Oh, dear, don't say that. Monte Vinha is a beautiful town. You always said so. I thought someday you and the kids were going to come back and run the café."

"Not anymore, we're not. Let's go. You're coming with me." Brigida put her arm around her mother, urging her toward the funny orange vehicle. "Wait in the car with Rute and Zezinho while I go inside and take care of things."

"I guess I can come for a visit," Dona Mafalda murmured, smiling as they passed me on the way to the curb.

Two young children were now peering at us from the car, their noses pressed against the window. A boy and a girl, maybe a year or two apart, both preschoolers.

"Don't let them out of the car," warned Brigida with the voice of someone who expected to be obeyed. "And don't tell them about Papa . . . I'll talk to them later."

Once Dona Mafalda was inside the car, her daughter strode purposefully toward the hospital, her fists clenched at her side. I stepped in her way.

"Oh!" she said, apparently having already forgotten I existed.

"Please. What's going on?"

Her jaw clenched and her nostrils flared. "What happened is that my father died today."

"He was sick?" Her father had to be the man we'd found outside the villa, which explained why he'd been there in the first place.

My comment enraged her. "No, he wasn't sick! At least not with anything the doctors could find. I talked to one of them on the phone, and he said my father was simply old, but both his parents and grandparents lived passed their nineties, and he has four older brothers, all still in great health. He was only sixty! But this town is cursed—hardly anyone makes it to seventy."

She had to be wrong, of course. Living in another town meant she wouldn't have kept up with all the residents. "Has anyone else you know here died?"

"Of course—that's the problem."

"How many?" Maybe she was talking one or two more.

"Let me see. There was Dona Ana, Senhor Gato, the eye doctor, the guy who ran the bakery by our house . . ." Her fists unclenched and her fingers popped out as she spoke each name. "Then my friend Monica's parents and Fatima's father and what's-his-name's uncle—I can't remember his name, but we're all friends on Facebook—"

By the time she ran down the list, she had used the fingers of both hands—twice.

"Are these older people? In their sixties? Fifties?"

"Sixties, like my father. They have children and grandchildren. It seems every day there's a new death. My friends and I talk about it all the time."

"Do they get sick first? Go to the hospital?"

"Sometimes. But mostly they just . . . slow down and don't wake up one morning."

She could be describing old age. "So no one else is getting sick? No children?"

"Not that I've heard about." Her eyes widened. "Are you saying the old people are dying? Is it some kind of virus?"

I wasn't suggesting that, but from what she was describing, a virus was a possibility. Except viruses that affected the old often affected children too. Then again, whatever experiments the Emporium was conducting in their fields might eventually kill everyone. Maybe older residents were only the beginning.

"Do-do-do you think it's going to spread? Oh, dear Lord." She looked heavenward and crossed herself. "My mother might already be sick. Maybe that's why she never gets upset when her friends die. She doesn't seem to really understand that her own husband is gone."

The woman looked ready to faint, and I put a steadying hand on her arm. "I saw an old man in the park today. He was fine. Just take your mother home with you and take care of her."

"Right, right." Her head bobbed up and down quickly, as if clamping onto my words. "I have to go inside and make arrangements for my father, but I'll take her back to Évora with me. I can't lose her. My children would be devastated. They're already going to miss their grandfather. He was their favorite." The tears I'd been expecting from her all along began to fall as her anger faded.

"I'm sorry for your loss." I hated seeing women cry. It made me want to melt metal or burst something into flames. Heat built inside my body, and I took my hand away before she felt it.

There was nothing I could do for her or her mother that she wasn't already doing, but I wished I could tell her I would fix the town. Problem was, where the Emporium was concerned, repairing what was wrong might not be possible because they didn't care about mortal casualties like we did. Still, even if it meant killing every last Emporium agent with my bare hands, I would try to make things right here.

"Thank you." She stepped around me and continued her journey into the hospital, wiping furiously at her wet face.

I glanced at Dona Mafalda to see how she was taking her daughter's orders to remain in the car. She sat there smiling, staring through the window with a blank expression and looking for all the world like a sweet grandmother. Apparently, whatever was insulating her from the death of her husband also made her accepting of Brigida's stronger will.

It was downright creepy.

The little boy had climbed into the front seat of the car and was playing with the steering wheel. His older sister still pressed her face against the window, her forehead wrinkled with concern. I hoped they told her sooner rather than later about her grandfather. A hundred and eighty years had taught me that the truth, however devastating, was better than wondering why the adults were suddenly acting crazy.

As I started to turn away, the girl's small hand came up to wave at me. I nodded and waved back, feeling a little silly but glad I did it when a smile replaced the worry on her face.

Back on my bicycle, I headed out of town, realizing that the plastic on the bike handles was melting away. I was also beginning to feel jumpy inside.

I needed to calm down—and I needed more curequick

from my pack. The cravings came faster each day, no matter how I tried putting them off.

That was when I noticed a guy on a moped following me. Not glancing again in his direction, I made a few turns just to make sure.

Yep.

And he didn't look Portuguese.

Losing a single tail might not be a problem, especially now that night was setting in. If there were others set up around the town, I might be in trouble.

It bothered me was that I had no idea how long the man had been following me. Since the hospital? Or maybe the two Portuguese Kenna and I had seen by the vineyard had reported us. Someone could have even spotted us dumping the old man's body, though they'd have to be better at tracking than Kenna to have tailed us that long.

But that really didn't matter. What did matter was if they had tracked me, Kenna might have been followed too.

CHAPTER 4

THE FIRST COURSE OF ACTION WAS TO LOSE THE TAIL. I stopped at a random pub to consider my options and called Kenna while I ordered a beer for cover.

No answer from Kenna. I sent her a text: *Tail.* That would say it all.

Why didn't she answer?

Casually, I scanned the café. The men and women looked like natives, most of their faces bronzed dark by the sun, and their vague smiles reminded me of Dona Mafalda. There was no loud laughter or drunken behavior that typically punctuated these places in the evening, though the night was still young. Not one person appeared over fifty.

A trip to the pub in Portugal was sometimes a family endeavor, but this town seemed to take that to extremes. Children were at almost every table, sitting as docilely as their parents.

Exactly what we'd seen during our first walk through the town, only more accentuated in this environment. I cranked my neck to see if my tail was still out there. He was, and he was chatting on a cell phone.

Great. I wasn't sticking around for his backup to arrive.

I downed the rest of my curequick-laced beer. Already I felt the buzz, soothing my jitters and enhancing my metabolism as it purged the alcohol from my system. Even without curequick, it was impossible for Unbounded to get inebriated with regular-strength alcohol, so at least I had clear senses going for me.

Outside, I jumped on my bike and started pedaling, wishing I'd taken the rental car. That reminded me of Kenna, who still hadn't answered.

I steered down a road, through a narrow alley, and into a park at the center of town. The problem with the moped was that he could go anywhere I could. My only advantage was that I could choose where to stop running. I slowed and let him catch up to me in the park. Night had fallen in earnest now, and given the inevitable confrontation, I was glad for the cover of darkness.

I slipped off my bike, but I didn't step away from it. The metal beneath my hands slowly heated. It wouldn't be long before the tires and seat melted. Would he even notice?

I waited until the man approached. He was grinning, but the expression was nothing like the vacant smiles in the pub. It was knowing and cruel, taunting. He was taller than me by a foot, and his hair was light brown, his eyes blue. With those pale features, he was definitely not native.

"Can I help you?" I said in Portuguese.

He paused, obviously not expecting me to sound like I belonged.

"What were you doing snooping around my fields today?" His Portuguese was fast, but heavily accented. He was English by the sound.

"I'm here on vacation. It's a lovely town."

"We don't get many tourists."

No, because the whole town is nuts, I thought. "That's too bad. It deserves more." I meant that literally. Everyone here deserved more than what the Emporium conglomerate had in store for them.

He stepped off his moped, still not going for a weapon, but the gleam in his eyes told me I'd been made. Maybe he detected the scorn in my voice instead of the fear he was accustomed to hearing. I doubted it. He didn't look that smart. More likely, his ability was combat and his instincts told him I was a serious threat.

I'd have to gamble on having the advantage of surprise. Otherwise, I might be the one roasted.

"So, what brings you to our town?" He jiggled the key to his moped in his left hand like a nervous tic.

"Your town?" It came out a half snort. "Oh, that's right—you said the fields were yours. But you don't sound native. How long have you lived here? A few months?"

His lips came together in a grimace that told me the

poor baby imagined he had a decent command of the language.

Closer, closer, I thought at him.

He obliged, his right hand moving toward the gun he'd have hidden at his back. I couldn't let him get too far.

Now. I released my grip on the bicycle.

The man instinctively put out his left hand to catch the handle where the rubber guard had long dripped to the ground.

His scream was instantaneous, as was the smell of searing flesh. Part of the handle bar came away, fusing with his hand. That he still managed to draw his gun said a lot about his skill and confirmed my suspicions about him being Unbounded. But the pain was too much even for him, and almost immediately, he curled over his wounded hand. The seat of the bike scraped his leg on the way down, smearing the hot remains of the padding and metal underneath.

His screams somehow grew louder. Definitely going to draw a crowd. My gun was already in hand, so I fired two shots into his torso. The screaming stopped.

Really, I'd done him a favor. If he was lucky, most of the damage caused by the molten metal would be healed before his heart started beating again. Depending on how much curequick he might already have in his body.

Furtively, I scanned the park for movement, but no one was running in my direction or shouting. I heaved a sigh of relief. Except I couldn't just leave him here. Even if no one stumbled on him tonight, he'd be found by morning when the women cut through the park on the way to Saturday market. The townspeople might be complacent, but they couldn't ignore an apparently life-less body in the middle of the walkway. But if I somehow managed to take him back to the villa, there was no guar-antee I could find and destroy his tracking chip before his comrades found him.

A greater concern was Kenna.

The thought of her decided me. For now, this guy could wait in the bushes. They were a little too sparse to hide much during the day but were adequate by night. It took only fifteen seconds to drag him to the densest area.

The bicycle was useless, but the moped was a better choice anyway. I ran to it, nearly colliding with a dark figure. At once my hands burned with readiness, my gift eager to be used. I reached out.

And stopped.

It was the old guy Kenna and I had seen earlier in the park. He stood in front of me dressed in a dark coat that draped on his thin frame. His gray hair was slightly askew, his face brushed with a day or two's growth of stubble.

How much had he seen?

Protocol indicated that I incapacitate him so he wouldn't jeopardize the op, but he looked just like my short, wizened grandpa, and there was no way I was going to punch him, or even drug him. For all I knew, I would accidentally kill the only aged person in the entire town.

"Keep quiet," I told him. "The whole town is at risk. I'm trying to fix it."

His dark eyes glittered in the moonlight, his face expressionless. He didn't reply but looked past me right at the bushes.

I was screwed.

Nothing I could do about it. Jumping onto the moped, I prepared to flee. Where was the stupid key? Belatedly I remembered it in the Emporium agent's left hand. No doubt it was part of the fused mess of my bicycle now.

The old guy was still watching me.

"Do you have a car?" I demanded.

His eyes went to my gun. I wasn't pointing it at him, but I would if I had to.

"Come with me," he said, his words garbled by either age or fear.

I followed him from the park and down a side street until we came to a squat motorcycle with a ridiculously huge, tightly-woven wicker basket bolted to a homemade frame on the back. Similar setups had once been more familiar in Portugal, their owners often stacking an entire pickup load of wares into these homemade baskets. If the situation had been different, I would have been amused at the quaintness.

Five large cardboard boxes half full of vegetables crammed into this particular basket. Interesting. Did the old man grow them himself or did he work for the Emporium?

He took a key from a ring and handed it to me. "I would like it back," he said, "when you are finished. Please."

I nodded. I was trying to protect humanity, but I was taking what was probably his entire livelihood. "I'll leave it here with the key in the basket."

He reached in and heaved out one of the boxes. "Room for the body," he muttered.

I wanted to tell him to stop, that I wasn't going back for the agent, but I had a few questions. Grabbing a box, I asked, "You're a farmer? You grow these?"

"All my life." He set down another box. "Used to do good business before that man and the others came." He jerked his head toward the park.

"They sell vegetables in town?"

A brisk nod. "If you can call it selling. They practically give food away. People won't buy my veggies anymore. I mostly take 'em to friends."

"You eat your own?"

He chuckled. "Of course. They taste better."

I doubted that—I'd eaten the grapes in the vineyard—but he was still alive. That was more than I could say for Dona Mafalda's husband and the others her daughter had listed.

"You never eat any of their food?"

He spat out his disgust. "I make it a point not to."

Which was good for me, since he didn't seem too concerned about reporting my assault.

"What about bread?" Surely the old man bought bread

here, and with all those wheat fields, the Emporium had to be selling flour locally as well.

"One of my cousin's sons owns a bakery, next town over. I go there twice a week."

We'd finished unloading the boxes, and I threw my leg over the motorcycle. "I would keep eating your vegetables," I said. "And that guy in the park? I don't have time to deal with him now, but if things work out, I'll be back for him."

"I hope before he wakes up."

I stared, forgetting whatever I'd been going to say next. Apparently the old guy was sharper than I'd given him credit. Sometime during the past years, he'd witnessed something he shouldn't have, and the Emporium's carelessness about keeping our existence a secret said volumes about the fate they planned for the town. I was betting no one was meant to survive.

Yes, they will.

I dipped my head to the old man, and kicked the engine to life. *I'm coming, Kenna,* I thought. Finally.

She'd better be okay, or I *would* be coming back for the Emporium agent, and he'd regret the day he'd Changed.

CHAPTER 5

I LEFT THE MOTORCYCLE A HALF MILE FROM THE VILLA AND ran the rest of the way. When I reached it, the place was utterly dark. A sedan that didn't belong sat outside the house next to our rented one with no sign of an occupant. Dread crawled across my shoulders.

Drawing my gun, I headed around the back. Kenna's bike was neatly stored on the cobbled deck where we'd found it—and in a lot better shape than mine. Everything looked peaceful, from the moon reflected in the rippling water of the swimming pool, to the whispers of the wind through the leaves of the trees lining the patio.

I didn't fool myself that Kenna was resting. If she'd finished here, she would have joined me in town. Besides, there was that little matter of the extra car sitting out front. I stepped to the back door. Sure enough, it was slightly ajar.

Dropping my pack to the ground by the door, I eased into the house, pausing just inside the door to allow my eyes to adjust to the dark. Already I could see evidence of a struggle. Two figures sprawled on the floor, the sofa was overturned and a swath of ripped fabric hung from its side. Everything else was too dark to see. I inched forward.

A dark figure hurtled at me from behind the couch. The next instant, a blow threw my gun across the room. My first punch was blocked, but I landed the second. So did my opponent. Breath rushed from me as pain spread across my chest. I kicked out, but nothing was there. A fist landed on my jaw from the other direction. I feigned right and punched left, but the blow only grazed my opponent, who'd dodged out of the way.

Combat Unbounded, I thought. No way for me to beat him without using my own ability.

Heat gathered in my hands. All I needed was to touch the Emporium agent for more than a few seconds and this would be over. Finding those few seconds, however, might be fatal.

I took two pounding blows, trying to find an opening. A third blow met my ribs with an agonizing *crack!* But exposing myself afforded the opportunity to latch onto an arm. My opponent struggled to pull away, gasping with pain. I held on. My whole body burned with heat.

"Blaze," the figure screamed. "Stop!"

Kenna.

Damn.

The next moment, we were falling, and I was sucking back the heat. It was easier to turn it off than to begin, but her grunts of pain as we fell told me I wasn't fast enough.

At last, she lay pinned under me, soft in all the right places.

I'd hurt her. "Are you okay?"

"Fine. *Get off!*"

Right. I rolled off her, clenching my jaw against the pain in my ribs. "Is anyone else here?"

"No. I took care of the last one right before you arrived. I thought you were their reinforcements." Her voice was faint, and her rapid breathing told me she was hurt badly.

"Do you think they called backup?"

"I don't know."

I left her side and crawled to the lamp that was on the floor next to the overturned sofa. Every movement sent needles of pain through my ribs and chest. As long as I took shallow breaths, the pain was bearable, but with my luck, I'd get to the stupid lamp and it would be broken.

Too slowly, I passed the two sprawled figures, both men, dressed in black from head to toe. They were definitely dead, at least for now. I'd need to secure them before they awoke. I reached the lamp, flipping the switch, and to my surprise, light flared into the room. I crawled back to Kenna, trying not to breathe too deeply.

Kenna still lay where I'd left her. Her wig was gone, revealing red hair pinned tightly to her head. A large section of her bare left arm was blackened, and I guessed the damage was deep enough to kill the nerves because she was moving the arm without sobbing. She'd need time to regenerate. The rest of her skin was only little reddened, so I hadn't damaged her anywhere else, but sometime during the evening, she'd taken a bullet in her thigh. How she'd managed to fight me at all was a testament to her ability.

Searching the room, I found a nine mil on the carpet—not mine or hers. I checked the magazine; six out of ten bullets left. "Here," I said, giving it to her before climbing painfully to my feet. "I'll get the kit." I was back in a minute, locking the doors and closing the shutters and curtains on the way. I wanted a warning if we had any more visitors.

From our medical kit, I took out several syringes of curequick mixed with pain killer. Deep wounds always benefitted from curequick injections, and she'd need them to get walking again. My hands shook as I fitted a needle.

I glanced to see Kenna watching me. "You'd better take some first."

Grimacing, I looked away, unable to meet her gaze as I tried to remember where I'd left the pack with my curequick. An injection into my bloodstream would be better for the pain, but in a way, it was nice to feel something besides the buzz from the curequick or the horrible aching need addiction left in my gut.

Kenna fished something from a pocket near her waist-band. "Here," she said, tossing it.

I barely caught the tiny pouch of curequick, flattened and still warm from her body. Nodding my thanks, I ripped the top open with my teeth and sucked it in.

My shaking easing, I injected her leg first, checking to see how bad it was. The bullet had gone in, but there was no exit wound. "I'm going to have to remove the bullet." Removing it would aid in healing, which we needed her to do fast.

"Give me two minutes. I won't feel anything by then."

She was right. Our pain killers had to be strong or they wouldn't stick around in our bodies long enough for surgery.

"I should have known it was you," she said as I made tiny injections around and in the blackened skin on her arm. She didn't flinch.

"Why's that?"

"You make a lot of noise."

I glanced toward the fallen men. "They didn't?" Why was she still alive then?

"No noise, but I stopped to look at the watering system on one of the other fields and caught a glimpse of them. No mistaking an Emporium hit team. So I came in the front and snuck around the back and waited for the one who tried to enter there. I would have had them both but . . . but . . ." Sudden moisture filled her eyes. She closed them, her expression becoming rigid, impassive.

"Did I hurt you?" I pulled out the empty needle.

She shook her head. "It's not that. The courier service sent a woman, but the other Emporium agent picked the front lock, and he was inside when she arrived. He answered the door, let her in, probably thinking it was me. I didn't get to her in time." Her gaze strayed to her leg, and I guessed she had taken the bullet trying to save the woman.

"Where is she? Maybe . . ." Standing, I saw the very young woman dressed in khaki pants and a blue shirt. She was curled up on the other side of the sofa, one of the cushions obscuring half her body. A black bag lay open near her, papers spilled over the floor.

"She's gone," Kenna said before I could move toward the girl. "I was checking when you came." Her voice was devoid of emotion but somehow told me more than if she'd let the tears fall. "We're supposed to help mortals, not send them to their deaths."

I thought of the old man and knew exactly how she felt. I hadn't hurt him, but I would have if it had meant saving all the others in the town.

"I'm sorry," I said.

She nodded. "Me too."

A single silent tear strayed down her face. Swallowing hard, I turned and retrieved the sofa cushion that wasn't covering the courier and worked it under Kenna's head.

"You can only do what you can," I said.

When she didn't respond, I pushed on the edges of her gun wound with my finger. She didn't stiffen but looked away as I took a scalpel from the medical kit and cut into her leg deep enough to remove the bullet. I followed the extraction with a few stitches and a bandage.

She studied me as I scooted next to her on the floor. "It's not your fault, you know," she said.

"What?"

"The addiction."

"Of course it's my fault."

"You forget I've been a part of the ops. I've seen what Greggor and the others did to you, sending you in again and again. And you coming back dead or so damaged they had to submerge your entire body in curequick to get you to regenerate in time for the next op."

I couldn't look away from her mesmerizing eyes and those pale cheeks. "It was my choice. I knew the risk."

"You were in mourning."

I didn't need to tell her what it had done to me to watch my wife age and die. In her lifetime, Kenna had already experienced that same loss. Older Unbounded said it got easier.

"They should have given you more time between ops."

"Maybe."

Grimacing with pain, she moved toward me until our bodies touched along the length of our sides. "Not maybe. Definitely. The fact that they keep sending you proves you're capable, but I think they've pushed you too far. After this, you have to tell them no. You have to take care of yourself first. You need to get free."

She was so beautiful. I wanted to kiss each of those

freckles, taste her lips, explore her body. I wanted to eat grapes off the vine and take her to the second house I owned on the Portuguese coast. It would never happen unless I was free.

"Okay," I said.

She rested her head on my shoulder, and I slipped an arm around her, gently pulling her closer. My chest felt tight. How long had I wanted to hold her this way? Even this afternoon the idea was out of reach, but now staying this way forever seemed like a possibility.

Except it wasn't. Kenna needed a few more minutes to heal and for a little of the numbness to recede before we could move, but in the meantime, we had to come up with a plan.

I dragged my attention back to our situation. "I was followed too." I told her about Dona Mafalda's daughter, the man on the moped, and the old guy in the park. "I think they've genetically modified the food. To kill. I don't know if it's a poison or a virus or something else altogether, and I have no idea why it's killing older people, or if there are other casualties we aren't aware of."

"But the Emporium is going to need mortals in the new world they want to create. A virus might kill too many workers the Emporium would need to provide special services."

"Yes, but they don't need old people—and they won't need mortals forever. Without the war between Renegades and Emporium, we'll multiply, and sooner or later our longer lives mean we'll far outnumber mortals. Then the Emporium won't need any of them."

"But even with genetic manipulation, only half our offspring Change."

"Exactly. More than enough to fill any grunt position. The Emporium has never been above using their own children."

Kenna looked thoughtful. "If you're right, the Emporium plans to have mortals work until whatever is in that food does its job and kills them. The money saved on health care alone would be astronomical."

"And you've seen how weird everyone is here. Docile, absently friendly, smiling at everything."

"No rebelling. No protest."

"Exactly."

"We have to stop it."

"They'll be coming for us," I countered.

"I know. Let's call Greggor for a quick update; he's waiting for our report. I only need a minute or two more. I should be able to move then."

"Even if he can send backup, they won't get here in time."

"I know."

I put in my password and dialed the number. Nothing. "There's no cell service."

"Try the laptop. Maybe you damaged your phone when you melted the bicycle."

I had a feeling it couldn't be that easy. It never was when we went head-to-head with the Emporium.

Leaving Kenna, I went to retrieve my laptop. Already I was breathing a little easier, and by tomorrow, my ribs wouldn't even twinge.

My laptop appeared miraculously undamaged on the floor by the coffee table, and as I reached for it, I couldn't help seeing the face of the courier. She looked so young, so peaceful, despite her violent death. We'd have to make sure her family was taken care of, if she had any.

Seated again next to Kenna, I attempted to link to the Internet over my laptop's internal data connection, while she patted herself down, looking for her phone.

"Nope," I said. "Not working either."

"Then I guess it won't help to find my phone. I was trying to text you when I got busy with those agents. I've no idea where it ended up. We'll try the satellite connection when we get outside, if they haven't blocked that too." She rotated up onto the knee of her good leg. "Let's go."

I wanted to protest that she wasn't ready, but I knew it didn't matter. We'd already stayed too long. When these Emporium agents didn't report in, someone would come looking for them. Besides, combat Unbounded were better than the rest of us at pushing through the pain.

At that moment we heard the chopper.

We were too late.

CHAPTER 6

KENNA WAS UP BEFORE I WAS, REACHING FOR THE GUN I'D given her earlier and dragging her wounded leg behind her. I hit the destruct button on my laptop, snatched up another gun, and barely beat her to the back door. "We have to get into the trees," she said. "Before they trap us."

I yanked open the sliding glass door and put one arm around her waist, the other arm scooping her legs out from under her before she could protest. Without checking the sky, I ran from the house, carrying her. Bullets sprayed us from the approaching chopper, but they were still too far away to be accurate. My ribs screamed, and every bruise Kenna had given me in our fight burned with renewed pain. I pushed myself harder.

With relief, I watched the trees rise up before me. Kenna struggled in my arms, and I let her down before she broke any more of my bones, keeping my arm around her waist for support. The trees were planted too far apart to be decent cover, but at least they gave us something to dart in and out of as we headed for the denser patch of wild olive trees farther in.

I glanced back once and saw men perched on the edge of the chopper, rifles in hand.

Something sliced into the fleshy part of my upper right arm, and agony rippled through my body. From long habit, I bit down hard on a scream.

We made it to the thicker grove, where the heavy brush between the trees afforded better cover but made our flight more difficult. I half carried Kenna as we fought our way through, and it became clear that I wasn't the only one hit. Kenna's arm was also bleeding where she'd been grazed. No time to take care of either of us.

"Wait," she said after a moment. "They'll be dropping men to come after us. We need transportation they won't expect. Otherwise, we won't be fast enough to escape."

The old man's motorbike came to mind. It wouldn't go fast, and with the basket it was an awkward ride—not to mention a substantial target, but it would be better using it on the open road than traversing the countryside on foot.

"I left a motorcycle half a mile from the house, but in the other direction, on the way to town." Even as I spoke, I didn't know if she could make it that far fast enough to stay ahead of them.

"Let's backtrack and then circle around for it. We might be able to temporarily throw them off our trail."

"I've got a better idea." I held up my hands. "Let's make a distraction."

She nodded. "Okay, wait until I tell you."

"Yes, boss," I mocked, but without any bite in the words. Her guess would be more accurate than anything I could come up with.

We retraced our steps until we could hear the men moving through the brush, then we angled off to the left. We'd stumbled along exactly two minutes in the new direction when she stopped us. "Here. Do it here."

Releasing her, I squatted and rubbed my hand over some brush, dry from a long hot summer. In seconds, the heat transferred and the vegetation burst into flames. A bit of fire raced up my arm, singeing the hair, but I rubbed it out and repeated the process on the next clump of bushes, working in a line. Flames crackled, gobbling up the dry patches first before spreading to the greener bushes and trees.

Kenna touched my shoulder. "Enough."

Right. The flames were moving in all directions, coming dangerously closer. I put an arm around her and we ran.

Her leg seemed less numb now as the drugs worked through her body, but that meant more pain, and all this running was only making her wounds worse. My own arm and shoulder throbbed and there was enough blood that I'd need to tie it up soon. My shirt would do the trick for both of us once we got a chance to stop.

The end of the trees came sooner than expected.

Smoke filled our lungs, making it difficult to breathe, but my anxiety lessened when I spied the old man's motorcycle behind the tree where I'd abandoned it. Ripping off my shirt, now damp with sweat, I handed it to Kenna and dug for the keys in my pocket. Blood dripped down my arm to the ground, and shaking was already setting in. For the first time in a very long time I didn't have my pack or any curequick with me. My mouth went dry at the thought.

Wordlessly, Kenna ripped my shirt, tying a folded strip around my upper arm. I tore off another strip and fastened it around the blood seeping from her arm. Already I could see pink skin eating away at the edges of her burn on the same limb, but the healing wasn't coming fast enough for either of us.

She mounted the bike, taking control, and I climbed on behind her. Kenna's faster reflexes made her the best choice for driving, while I could cover us with the gun I'd taken from the villa.

On the dirt road, out of the trees, we were a clear target, but we reached the end of the road without incident and turned onto the paved one, heading out of town. Part of me regretted the choice to run from the Emporium agents, even while I knew it was the only responsible option. We had to regroup and decide what to do. Since we'd been compromised, I suspected Kenna would make the call to retreat and wait for backup, no matter how she felt about it personally.

It wasn't a terrible decision. While our mission hadn't

exactly been a success, we had an idea of what we were up against, and our Renegade cell could make an intelligent decision about how to proceed. Even if the Emporium took all their research and began again elsewhere, they no longer had the element of secrecy.

The downside was that we still didn't have a clear idea of what the Emporium was doing here or why this area was so important to them. Without knowing more about their experiments, we might not be able to help the townspeople who were already damaged. Understanding what was in the food and how long the townspeople had consumed it would make it easier to stop the progression and possibly reverse the damage. It would also help us know what to look for the next time the Emporium set up shop to experiment on mortals.

Thoughts banged around inside my brain, pushing to be heard, but that contrasted with the surprisingly pleasant fragrance of Kenna's pinned hair and the feel of her body in front of me. Between her closeness and the pain, I could barely think.

As if on some sort of signal, Kenna eased off the gas. I scanned both sides of the road in search of what she must have spotted, but we were alone. She shifted into neutral with her bad leg and cut the engine altogether, her body tensing in reaction from the movement. We hurtled forward for another half minute before coming to a stop at the side of the road.

"What is it?" I asked, putting my feet down on either side of the bike to balance it, not trusting her leg.

"I think I see something up ahead." She reached into the pocket of her shorts for the small set of binoculars she'd used earlier. The idea of her hidden pockets brought me a sliver of hope. Maybe she had more curequick.

"Yeah," she said, peering through them. "Two trucks parked across the road. A car too. Can't see how many men, but I'm betting they're Emporium." She smacked the gasoline tank. "I bet they have all the roads covered. And any other likely exit points. No easy way for us to get out of town. Looks like we've made right bags of this op."

Meaning we'd messed up. She was right about that, but testing the populace and the produce in the fields would reveal a lot, so maybe we'd done enough.

Or maybe that was my need for curequick talking.

"We just need to stay clear until Greggor realizes we've missed our report and sends backup," I told Kenna. I wasn't sure who he could send, but we had enough Renegade allies in Europe that he would manage to round up an able crew.

Scowling, she offered me the binoculars, then swung her good leg over the motorbike and stood a bit awkwardly, still holding onto one handlebar. "They're looking this way, but I don't think they've identified us yet. Must have heard the motorbike. We can hide in the trees until we decide what to do."

I knew she was waiting for me to move the bike, but I was staring at the familiar orange car in front of the trucks. The bubble-fronted vehicle was parked askew in the middle of the right lane, as if halted abruptly. It didn't look like anyone was inside.

One of the men broke away from the others and started toward us. Time to go.

I returned Kenna's binoculars and began pushing the motorbike into the trees. They'd be able to track us if they looked hard enough, but given the distance, they might assume we'd driven back the way we'd come. If it came to it, I could always start another fire to mask our trail.

"We might not be the only ones they're preventing from leaving," I said to Kenna. "Remember Dona Mafalda's daughter? That little orange car looks exactly like hers. You think they stopped her because the guy following me saw us talking?"

"Maybe, but if it's only about keeping everyone here, why not just make her turn around? Why is the car still there?"

I had no answer except that Brigida had probably put up some kind of fuss about not being allowed to leave, and the Emporium hadn't reacted well.

My fault. I should have soothed Brigida's worries, not asked questions that emphasized them. For all I knew, she and her family were lying dead on the floor of that car. Except there was no obvious damage to the vehicle—and the Emporium had never been known for "neat" kills.

Kenna let out a sigh. "The way they've come at us, I don't think the Emporium is going to back down. Even if they catch us, they know it won't be long until our people come to find out what happened."

A thought stopped the reply on my lips. "That old guy in the park? He knew the agent I killed would regenerate."

"So the Emporium hasn't been careful about hiding their abilities." Kenna's voice betrayed her anger. "That means they don't intend to leave. No wonder they've locked down the city. My guess is they'll either fortify the town with more agents so we can't get close, or they'll destroy the entire town."

Leaving no witnesses, and no people or crops to test.

I'd fought against the Emporium long enough to know their methods, but shock struck me anyway at her words. The people in this town were my kinsfolk. *Mine.* And this was my fight.

I took a steadying breath before saying, "The daughter knows something's going on here, and she was vocal about it. She had two kids with her." In my mind, I could still see the girl, her hand lifted in a trusting wave. The thought that she might never go home to her father, that she'd likely not survive the coming battle, made me ill.

Kenna gave me a sympathetic glance. "I was hoping the agents would be slow to realize the threat, but it seems I underestimated them."

"We can't let this happen," I said. "Those townspeople are like children themselves."

"You know the protocol. We don't have a choice. I'm sorry."

I knew she was.

We stumbled through the increasingly dense foliage, mostly bushes and an occasional olive or oak tree. We couldn't see the road now, so this was as good a place as any to stop and talk.

The faint sound of a siren reached our ears. "Looks like they're responding to the fire at least," Kenna said. "That's a sign they'll be fighting for control of the town, not running."

"In the end, it'll all be the same to the people."

"I know."

I came to a stop and faced her. "I have to go back."

"No you don't."

"I can't let them hurt those kids. Or the town."

She stared at me for a long moment as the darkness pressed in around us, her face only half lit by the overhead moon. Being a combat Unbounded, she had final say in our tactics, but I was going whether she agreed or not. Finally, she said, "You're a good man, Blaze Vincent."

I wasn't so sure of that, but I'd be damned if I'd stand by in relative safety while Dona Mafalda's family was being held somewhere by the Emporium because of their connection to me. These people were simple country folk, and the Emporium had no business messing in their lives.

"I'll cause more distractions," I told Kenna. "That'll keep them busy until you can contact Greggor and arrange backup. That way the Emporium won't have time to plan a resistance." I extracted my phone from my pocket, showing her the passcode that would open it without triggering the self-destruct. "Even if you can't make it to a place where you have service, Greggor should still be able to track your chip once they get close enough. Then you can all come for me. I'll meet you here, if I can."

Kenna pocketed my phone with barely a glance. "I'm going with you."

If the situation were reversed, I'd never let her go alone either, but this was my element. I'd successfully completed many similar ops. Going in as a distraction while the rest of the group carried out the real mission. Blocking the fear with swigs of curequick, not really caring what happened to me. Maybe even hoping, just a little, that the end would come swiftly.

I forced a smile. "We could both get caught."

She swallowed hard, and for a moment I was distracted by the motion of her throat and by the expression in her eyes. I wanted to kiss her, to trace her throat with my mouth, to taste her lips. Maybe she'd even let me.

No. I wouldn't try. The bullet wound and my body's struggle to repair the damage had increased my ever-present desire for curequick, and the yearning made me unsteady. The fear the curequick buzz normally kept in check careened rampant through my brain like some kind of crazy game of table tennis. She'd feel that I wasn't okay if I got close. She'd remember what kind of man I really was.

Kenna's face was unyielding. "We're partners. Together we have a better chance of finding what we came for—and more chance of getting away if we get caught."

Partners. We were that. I felt it as I hadn't with anyone else for years. "Okay."

We trudged back through the trees with the motorcycle, angling farther down the road in the direction of the villa. Kenna seemed to be walking with more ease now, which boded well for our new focus.

A cloud drifted over the moon, plunging us into darkness. Still, I saw her in my mind, the length of her throat, her eyes delving into mine. Tomorrow, maybe I'd kiss her.

If either of us were still alive.

CHAPTER 7

ALREADY I WAS PUSHING BACK THE JITTERS THAT TEMPTED me to curl up on the ground and howl like some rabid dog. So far, we hadn't run into any sign that we'd been pursued, but I was beginning to worry about how we'd get to Dona Mafalda and her family.

"The Emporium could be keeping them anywhere," I said. "*If* they've taken them." There was a chance they hadn't, but only a very slim one because of the abandoned car.

Kenna's head shifted in my direction, though I couldn't make out her features. "The only area we've seen them guarding is the compound near the vineyard. I'd say that's the best place to start. It's probably also where they're keeping their records." Kenna might care about helping me find Dona Mafalda's family, but her mention of the records told me she also hoped to complete our original mission.

Getting to the Emporium's compound meant at least a mile to town and another few miles beyond. With my wounds, walking was torture, and I suspected Kenna was experiencing a similar pain. Using the motorcycle might be worth the risk of the Emporium hearing us, but the basket made it impossible to drive through the trees, unless we traveled close to the road where the vegetation was sparse. Closer to the road was infinitely more dangerous.

I could remove the basket, but there was only one way to do that without tools, and that included the possibility of exploding the gas tank and ruining our only means of transportation. If only I weren't shaking so badly.

"We're wasting time," Kenna said, apparently coming to the same decision. She stopped walking and went down on her good knee. "You can melt the bolts holding this basket, right? Without blowing it up?" Trust her to get right to the point.

"Maybe. You have any curequick?" I hated to ask.

A quick shake of her head. "All back at the villa. I gave you the only pouch I had on me."

"Right." Forcing a smile, I squatted and peered under the motorcycle. *Steady,* I thought, reaching out a finger to the first of the four huge nuts. It melted without incident, followed by the second.

I was reaching for the third when a sudden crack of a branch made me careless, and the nut melted in a rush, liquefying also the bolt and the metal plates protecting the wicker, and leaving a fist-size hole in the basket itself. So much for my promise to the old man.

"This way! I hear something!" a voice called. Maybe in English or German—I was in too much of a hurry to do anything more than understand the meaning. Definitely not Portuguese.

Kenna drew her gun, placing her body between me and the voices. Leaving the last nut intact, I jumped on the motorcycle and started the engine. Kenna hopped on behind me, one hand wrapping around my bare chest as I popped the clutch, almost throwing us off the seat with the abruptness. The basket bounced, sending the three loose bolts flying.

I caught a glimpse of two men and assault rifles in my peripheral vision. I pushed harder on the gas, hurtling us forward through the trees. The basket twisted to the side, slamming into a tree and then back again.

Shots rang out after us, and Kenna fired back, emptying her entire magazine before turning to reload. The gun was one an Emporium agent had dropped at the villa and the magazine was different from her own, so she couldn't just slam in a new one from her endless pockets. By the time she'd reloaded the magazine, the men were long behind us.

I headed for the open road, urging the old bike to its limit, the engine screaming under the strain. The horizon in the direction of the villa was aglow, but not raging, so they must have the blaze under control. I was glad for that; I didn't want to hurt any of the Portuguese residents.

The expectation of seeing headlights from an

Emporium truck behind us was so great it was almost a relief when they finally appeared. I was nearly at the town, which was strangely deserted, though everyone must have heard the fire engines. I drove into an alley and out the other side, losing the black truck but running into another one two streets later.

I screeched to a sliding stop, turning as we skidded toward the truck. Shots fired from the windows, one ricocheting off the gas tank. The basket, still attached by that one bolt, jerked to one side and back again. Kenna let off only one return shot this time, apparently preserving ammunition.

Tearing down another alley, we came out just in front of a third truck. They were closing in on us now. More shots had me ducking and tensing for a possible impact.

If they caught us, they would kill us—but not permanently. Not yet. I would only wish they had. No, they'd torture us for information and breed us for our talents. Keep us in a locked cell for decades or centuries until they had no use for us. Then they would chop us up, severing the three focus parts of our bodies. A final death.

Neither of us would go easily. Kenna let off another shot, blowing a tire on the truck behind us.

Only two more streets. There. I could see the end of the town. If I could make it to the countryside, the trucks wouldn't be able to follow so fast through the trees, and we might stand a chance of reaching our target. One truck was still hot on our tail, and I glimpsed another on a parallel road through the side streets. To my left, the swift river and the three-foot wall bordering it cornered me every bit as much as the trucks.

But the way in front was still clear.

Then it wasn't. A dark truck squealed to block the end of the street, men with rifles piling from the back. No way could we run that gauntlet. I had my gun, and Kenna had whatever bullets were left in hers, but they would be useless against so many.

That left only one option.

I swerved sharply to the right and then to the left, gunning the engine. Kenna's hands dug into my sides. Seconds seemed to turn into minutes as we careened toward the short wall that bordered the river. With a sickening screech, metal ground into concrete. The impact sent us flying up, up, and over—into the rushing water. The bike stayed behind on the road, but the wicker basket, finally shaken loose, came splashing into the water after us.

More shots peppered the river. Kenna dived, and I followed, letting the water bury me and carry me away. Unbounded could absorb oxygen from the water, so we could stay under longer than the average mortal, but after twenty or thirty minutes, we'd eventually lose consciousness and surrender to the water.

The river was swifter and colder than I'd expected, and scattered rocks along the bottom battered at me as I passed. When I finally came up, trucks, town, and bullets had been left behind. The *whomp-whomp* of a chopper reached my ears, but it was still some distance away by the sound.

"Grab on," Kenna called.

She clung to the damaged remains of the wicker basket, and I reached for it myself, floating with the current for a few blissful minutes. The basket was definitely the best option to keep afloat and preserve energy for now. I might even be growing fond of the stupid thing.

The adrenaline blasting through my body had temporarily masked my need for curequick, but the craving would return soon, and I needed to remain strong. And warm. My ability couldn't heat the entire river, but I could heat the water around me, even turn some of it into steam, if needed. Letting off only a bit of energy, I heated the water immediately around us so our muscles wouldn't lock up with the cold.

Kenna threw me an amused glance, telling me she'd noticed, but she didn't comment.

The sounds of the chopper faded—a good sign, I hoped. The river would take us closer to the vineyard, but I knew from studying the layout earlier that it veered off before reaching the buildings. We needed to get out before then—and on the left side.

As the adrenaline rush eased, my shaking increased. The bend in the river approached, and Kenna took off swimming in an angle toward the bank, but I waited a second too late. I struggled, the rush of water pulling me past the bend. Maybe I'd drown after all, and the Emporium would be waiting with an interrogator when I revived.

No.

I took a deep breath and plunged into the water, pushing outward with my hands until the water around me boiled, steaming away like water in a pan on the stove. In that instant, I pushed against the river bottom and drove myself upward, popping out of the water and catching onto the branch of a scraggly tree growing halfway down the bank.

Crawling onto solid ground, I collapsed, sucking in air and pulling back my gift before I melted the earth and rocks and set fire to the forest. The shaking in my body grew worse, and so did my pain. All I wanted was another swig of curequick so I could do my job.

Only the image of the little girl waving at me from the car urged me to my feet, to join Kenna at the top of the bank. "Ready to do this?" she asked, seeming remarkably chipper in the face of our dire circumstances.

This. It was what we were born to do—fight, protect, serve.

"Yeah." I unholstered the gun I'd taken from the villa, hoping it still worked after my dip in the river, and started forward. My stumbling pace eventually worked into an awkward jog. Kenna was no longer even limping.

Reaching the vineyard, we bent over and crept to the last row of vines. My gut twisted in protest and my internal voice told me to wait until backup arrived. But I had a vested interest in these people, and Dona Mafalda's little family in particular.

Kenna had lost the binoculars in the river, but we couldn't see anyone patrolling this section of the fence.

Maybe all their guards were out searching for us. These buildings were probably the last place they expected us to go. Crawling on my belly, I made it to the fence, reaching out to melt enough of it to open a good-sized hole.

So far, so good.

"Which building?" Kenna asked.

"I doubt they have a place to keep prisoners in the storage barns or processing facilities. So I'm guessing there." I pointed to the squat building we'd seen guards going in and out of earlier. The yellow paint on the building's stucco looked a dull gray in the darkness.

"As good a place as any to start." Kenna lead the way, sprinting across the open space to the yellow building. I followed with a lot less grace.

We found a darkened window toward the back. Kenna stood watch as I heated the glass, feeling it start to buckle under my touch.

With a warning hiss, Kenna tugged me back from the window. She jerked her head in the direction of two guards swaggering toward the building next door where the cabbage workers had unloaded their harvest.

Pressing myself to the ground close to the building, I gripped my gun and waited until they disappeared inside. My head buzzed with a need that was growing harder to ignore. I had to hurry and finish this.

Kenna gave the all clear, and I climbed to my feet. Reaching out to the window, I finished heating the glass, sending a molten mass dripping down both sides of the sill, glowing with the intensity of my ability.

As we waited for it to cool, another guard rounded the building, giving a surprised shout as Kenna launched herself toward him. Her movements were liquid and sure, but the Emporium agent met her stroke for stroke.

Combat Unbounded, I thought, watching this strange and deadly dance.

Kenna spun and offered a final kick in the stomach that sent him careening backwards into the building. His head slammed into the stucco with an echoing *crack!* As he slid down the side into a messy heap, Kenna bent over him, her hands coming up with a gun and more ammo.

Climbing through the window, we found ourselves in a small, deserted kitchen. Kenna raced across the room toward the door, opening it to reveal a narrow dimly-lit hallway. No one in sight. Kenna took two steps, but jumped back before I could follow. Her hand signaled for silence.

Clop, clop, clop. Measured footsteps came down the hall. A man spoke, his voice soon joined by two others, the tones urgent. More footsteps. We waited, my heartbeat sounding like a drum in my ears. This time the adrenaline didn't seem to take even the edge off my craving.

Far too soon, Kenna moved forward in a blur, shooting a woman and sending a man to the ground with a few choice kicks. I pushed the remaining man against the wall, my gun pointed at his pale face.

"Don't move," I ordered in English, almost hoping he'd disobey so I could shoot him.

"Okay! Okay. Don't shoot!" His entire body shook.

"Your people stopped two women with a couple kids trying to leave town," I said. "Where are they?"

"I don't know what you're talking about." His glance strayed to his fallen companions. "Please don't hurt me," he pleaded. "I'm mortal. Not like them. Please, don't kill me."

He was probably telling the truth. The Emporium typically employed more mortals than Unbounded, and though their leaders normally chose Unbounded for the most important ops, they always needed someone to make coffee and clean their toilets.

Kenna put her hand over his throat, bringing her face close to him. "I'm giving you two seconds to tell us where they are, or I *will* shoot you."

"Someone said something about a woman and some kids over the radio an hour or so back. I don't know anything more, I swear! There isn't a woman here. I would know."

Kenna seemed to accept that. "The Emporium is killing people here. How?"

"I-I-I don't know."

"Wrong answer." Kenna pushed harder against his neck, making him gasp for air. "Another wrong answer, and I'm going to put a bullet in your leg—and then in every other part of your body until you tell the truth. What are you doing here? It's in the crops. That much we know. Is it a disease? Some kind of virus?"

The man gagged, his breath coming in huge panicked

gasps. I didn't blame him. Kenna was scary—it was downright awesome.

"Not disease. The crops have been engineered to enhance a few natural toxins. I-I don't know the science. I just manage the harvest workers." He paused, as if waiting to see if that was enough information.

Kenna pointed her gun at his thigh. "And?"

His voice rose to an annoying squeal. "It accumulates in everyone who eats it—mortals, I mean." A slight curl of his lips hinted that he might not be as content with this as he might have led his employers to believe. Of course, that would be a matter of self-preservation. One never left Emporium employ, unless it was in a casket.

"It kills all mortals?" I asked.

He shook his head. "Mostly it depresses the neurotransmitters in the brain. I don't know the science, but it makes people calm. It's only fatal to older people as their organs age. Their systems can't handle the accumulation—but that's a sign they are becoming less effective anyway."

I sneered. "So you murder them."

"It's better than other alternatives," the man said, his eyes haunted. Sweat sheened across his forehead. "Believe me."

"You're sure it doesn't kill anyone else?" Kenna asked the question before I had the chance.

"Well, there is also a fifty percent higher fatality rate in the babies of the women who consume—"

Kenna's grip on his throat must have increased because

he choked off and his face, even in the dim light, was bright red.

"Please!" he gasped.

Kenna eased off and leaned forward to speak in his face. "You're going to help me get the crop information. Now."

His eyes darted wildly. "I don't know the computer password! I don't have access to the print records."

"I'll get access. You show me where."

He flung out his left arm. "Down that way. The office."

Kenna pulled him from the wall, grabbing the back of his shirt. To me, she said. "Look for Dona Mafalda and her family. I'll get the records."

Without seeming to look, she fired down the hall as a figure rounded the bend. "They'll track us here eventually," she added. "We don't have much time. Get out as soon as you find them or determine they aren't here. I'll meet you in the vineyard."

Our captive turned slightly toward us, stiffening as he hit the barrel of her gun. "Try the barns. They sometimes sport with locals there."

"Get going." Kenna pushed at him.

I went back inside the dark kitchen. Kenna would check rooms here as she went, clearing a path to the office, and if she found the family, she'd get them out. My best bet was to do as the mortal agent had said and search the other buildings.

I had almost reached the melted window when a terrified scream shot through the night.

CHAPTER 8

*K*ENNA! WAS MY FIRST THOUGHT. BUT KENNA WOULD DIE before she gave that kind of satisfaction to an Emporium agent. No, the scream was coming from outside, and I was guessing it was Dona Mafalda or Brigida.

I sprinted the remaining steps to the window and peered out into a deceptively quiet night. The faint stench of smoke filled the air, but there were no guards in sight. Another high-pitched scream split through the calm, coming from the cabbage barn the two guards had entered earlier when we'd arrived. I vaulted through the window and darted across the open space, expecting at any minute to feel the hot slice of a bullet piercing my body. But I reached the barn doors in safety—and none too soon. Two of the black trucks were rolling through the main gate, stopping out of my sight behind the stuccoed building. Kenna was about to have more visitors.

Nothing I could do to back her up. Not with the

panicked cries and whimpers now leaking from the barn. I pulled one of the massive doors open a crack and peered in. Not more than a car length away, a guard gripped Brigida's arm, keeping her in place while the other guard held his gun to her little boy's head. The child stood on unsteady feet, crying for his mother, but each time he tried to go to her, the guard pushed him back with the gun. The little girl clung to her mother's leg, whimpering.

"Please," Brigida said in broken English. "I no know this man. I see him today. I no know anything. Please, please, no hurt my baby!"

"If you got nothing to tell us, we don't need any of you." The guard jabbed his gun into the boy's head, sending him sprawling backwards onto the ground. The child's scream was garbled with tears.

"I don't know," the other guard said with a smirk at Brigida, jerking her back as she tried to run to her sobbing child. "She's awfully pretty."

"So are dogs," retorted the other. "But you do whatever you want. I'll get rid of the kids."

"No!" Brigida cried.

I fired, hitting the man with the gun in the forehead. He crumpled at the same time Brigida yanked away from the second guard, rushing to her son and snatching him up in her arms. The second guard pulled out his gun, aiming at me, but I was already firing. One bullet slammed into his left shoulder. The second shot brought only a *click!*

Grinning insanely as if he didn't notice the bullet, the

guard pulled his trigger. I dove to the side, heating and throwing my gun at him. I missed his face, the molten metal hitting his chest instead. He screamed but didn't retreat, his leather jacket apparently protecting too much of his skin. Lunging at him, I punched hard at his face, leaving a deep burn across his cheek.

His returning jab to my ribs felt like being hit with a sledge hammer. Biting down on the pain, I drew closer, slamming him with first one fist and then the other. His clothing and skin blackened wherever I touched. He fought back with viciousness, his hands blurs that barely registered in my vision. He knew the places to hit that would bring the most pain and struck relentlessly. Blackness threatened to plunge me into unconsciousness, but I pushed it back, just like I did with the cravings. If I could hold on for just a few seconds more.

Blood dripped down my face, obscuring my vision. I lashed out, connecting with his jaw. The skin melted in a rush, burning away his entire face. His mouth opened in a scream—one he never uttered as he collapsed to the floor and lay there unmoving.

Brigida stared in horror, both children now in her arms, their faces pressed to her body. "You," she said hoarsely.

The heat seeped from me in a rush. "Where's your mother?" I asked her in Portuguese.

Brigida shook her head, her face crumpling. "She said she didn't know anything. They didn't believe her."

"I'm sorry. But you have to get out of here now."

Shouting outside told me it was already too late.

"Come on!" Jumping to my feet, I grabbed Brigida's shoulder. She resisted at first, but when I pulled her daughter from her arms, she stopped fighting me. We ran behind the large wagon the workers had used to haul the cabbages, coming up far too quickly against the wall. "Look for a door!"

"There's none. I looked earlier when they first left us."

Pushing the little girl at her mother, I strode to the wall, calling on my ability. It answered my demand, eager and willing. Almost immediately as I touched it, the wood burst into flame. Ignoring the renewed sobbing from the children and Brigida, I grabbed a shovel from the wagon and struck the burning wood until I cleared a hole large enough for them to exit. The fire spread faster, greedily consuming the dry wood.

I peeked outside and saw no one. "Get your kids out," I told Brigida. "There's a break in the fence leading into the vineyard. It's by one of the poles opposite the short building." I pointed in the general direction to be sure she understood. "Run to the fence and work your way up until you find it. Go into the vineyard. If you see a woman with red hair, you can trust her. No one else. If you don't see her, run as far away as you can. Hide until it's safe."

Would it ever be safe? Had Kenna even gotten out?

Brigida hesitated, her chest heaving. Behind us, both double doors burst open.

Brigida needed no more convincing. She bounded through the hole in the wall, as if the children in her arms weighed nothing more than a couple of kittens.

I turned back to the wagon, sending my heat into it. Between the blood drenching my face and the effects of my withdrawal, I was having trouble seeing, but my ability was working well. The wood of the wagon burst into flames, the metal parts beginning to melt. I pushed the entire thing in the direction of the oncoming men, hoping the wheels held up long enough to deliver my little surprise. Then I dived through the hole in the wall, summersaulting into a squatted position. Brigida was nowhere to be seen.

More shouting, but still no guards in sight. I headed for the next building, also setting it on fire. Kenna and I would be harder to catch if they were worried about saving their new buildings. They might even think twice about staying in Monte Vinha if they had to start completely over. I ran to the next building, tripping twice on my way and hitting the ground with a painful crunch. I was still having problem seeing. Bile rose in my throat.

The shouting was now accompanied by wailing sirens. Additional people arrived in trucks and began running around purposefully. Two strode in my direction, but I ducked behind the building I'd torched and hurried on. I risked melting two of the metal buildings, touching all the sides to hasten the collapse, and set fire to a third wooden barn. The last building I touched was an older one made of brick, and as heat funneled through it, the entire wall exploded in a rush of falling bricks and flaming debris, nearly trapping me in the process.

Coughing up smoke, I stumbled through the rubble to the fence and melted another hole, falling through it into a field of wheat. I was tempted to set it on fire as well, but I was already worried about Kenna, and about Brigida and her children. And the whole town.

Had my distraction been enough to save them from the Emporium? Or had I just hastened their deaths?

Every part of my body ached with agony. I crawled until I could no longer see the wheat around me.

Finally, I let myself collapse.

CHAPTER 9

ANGUISH PIERCED MY AWARENESS AND FORCED ME TO CRAWL from the blackness. I was on fire, pain filled my entire body, except my hands and feet, which felt blissfully numb.

Oh, God in heaven, please let me die.

"He's coming around," said a female voice. "Now that he's awake, we need to get him into the curequick."

Yes, dump me into an ocean of curequick. My body shook with need.

"No." The single word, spoken by a man, was completely unyielding. Somehow the voice was familiar, or maybe the tone, but I couldn't place it.

"He needs to heal," insisted the woman. "He's burned far too badly to give him much comfort otherwise. After he's better, we can worry about his addiction. It's too much all at once."

The man didn't back down. "Giving him curequick will only prolong his dependence. It's been five days since they found him. With our metabolism, five days is halfway there."

The blackness I'd crawled from invited me to return, but I clung to the familiarity of the man's voice. It was the only thing that seemed to cut through the cravings and the pain of . . . what? I didn't remember doing anything that could bring this agony.

"Not with his level of addiction, it isn't," the woman said. "Our bodies record the need for curequick in a way similar to how they record our memories even if our heads are severed—as long as our other two focus points, the heart and reproductive system, are intact. His recovery will take at least two months and maybe up to six."

"Look, I know your first priority as a doctor is to make your patient comfortable, but do not give him curequick, or you'll answer to me." The man's voice betrayed controlled anger, and I knew he had every intention of fighting for what he believed.

"I'm sorry, but my patient is an adult, and he has the final say." The doctor's voice moved closer. "Blaze, I'm Dr. Strout, I'm here to look after you. I can give you curequick with the sedative. Would you like that?"

I wanted to say yes. In fact, I wanted to beg for the curequick. But all at once I placed the other voice as that of my foster father. "Ritter?" I whispered. The effort sent shards of glass rippling down my throat.

"I'm here, Blaze. Your partner called me when they found you."

I struggled to open my eyes and could almost make out his face through a thick haze. "Where . . .?"

"You're in London. I flew here as soon as I heard."

That wasn't what I meant. "Kenna?"

"She's safe. You want me to get her?"

"No." The last thing I wanted was for her to see me like this.

There was more I wanted to know—about Brigida and her children, and the town. But my ability to even think had fled, and the torture I was experiencing cranked up a notch.

"Would you like the curequick?" The doctor asked again. "I wish I had an alternative to offer, but there isn't one. We can wean you off it later when you recover. It'll be easier then."

"Blaze, don't," came Ritter's voice, both firm and soft, punctuated by a pleading I hadn't heard from him for over a hundred and sixty-seven years.

I remembered the day he'd arrived in Portugal, standing in front of me with an uncertain expression as he explained that he'd been a friend of my grandfather's—great-grandfather's, I would find out later—and was there to take me with him to America. If I agreed.

I had. He had saved me then when I'd trusted him, and maybe he could help me now.

"No curequick," I said, the words barely a whisper from my parched throat. Never again.

As if to taunt me, the agony in my body became all encompassing. *I need it now!* I screamed inside my head.

"Give him a painkiller," Ritter ordered.

"It won't help. Not much. A sedative would be better, though it won't last."

"Give him both."

I didn't feel the prick of a needle, and it wouldn't have made a bit of difference if I had.

"You staying?" I asked Ritter.

"I'll be right here. You can do this, I promise."

From the moment he'd taken me in at thirteen, he'd kept every promise he'd made to me. Maybe I *could* do this.

The darkness threatened to take me, and this time I dived in.

TIME PASSED WITH THE EVER-CONSTANT, AGONIZING TORTURE, a need so deep I didn't know how I'd make it through another second. As my body healed from the burns, the demand for curequick increased tenfold. Every hour, I questioned my decision, but each time I thought to give in, Ritter was there, a barrier between me and any chance of curequick.

I lived for the moments of blessed unconsciousness, though these were haunted by images of a crying toddler screaming for his mother, and a little girl with a bullet hole in her chest.

Then after what seemed like an eternity, the haze partially lifted, like the dawn after a storm, and I awoke from a fitful sleep with only the familiar cravings instead of the blinding ones that made me want to curl into a ball and weep. I still wanted curequick—and quite badly—but it was nothing compared to the hell I had endured.

I looked over to see not Ritter but Kenna by my bedside, tucked in a chair, her red hair fanned over her face. Sleeping, she looked vulnerable, nothing like the tough warrior I knew her to be.

I must have made a sound because her eyes popped open, her hand sliding almost imperceptibly to her gun inside its holster. Without shifting position, she scanned the room until her gaze fell on me. Abruptly, she sat up. "Oh, you're awake."

I wanted to tell her to leave almost as much as I wanted to beg her to stay. The need to see her won out. "Was I dreaming, or was my father here?"

"Oh, he's been here nonstop until today. I finally made him leave to take a shower." She made a face. "Believe me, after seven weeks sitting in here, he needed it."

"Seven weeks," I mumbled. *Only seven?*

"I know. A long time."

I wasn't about to admit that it had felt like much longer. A year in purgatory would be a vacation after the past seven weeks.

"Ritter made me swear on my life to protect you from any offers of curequick. Though the doctor is just as happy as we are that you've made it this far."

Even the mention of curequick conjured a desire so strong I wanted to leap up and go find the drug myself. I pushed the need down, and to my surprise, it receded to a manageable level. "So, what happened in Portugal?"

A smile spread across her face. "You saved everyone, is what." She scooted the chair close enough that if I had been able to focus even a little bit better, I could have counted her freckles.

"I wasn't able to break through the codes on the Emporium's computer system with my limited tools," she went on, "but they had plenty in hard copy that I was able to steal, thanks to their preoccupation with your fires. Apparently, you destroyed nearly all the Emporium's buildings, including a brick one they were using as a lab. A good portion of their fields burned as well. Cities all around had to come help put out the fires. By the time Greggor and the reinforcements he called in from Italy arrived the next day, the Emporium was already pulling out. Best we can figure, they decided to cut their losses when they realized how far we—or you, rather—were willing to go to send them packing."

"The town burned?"

"The town lost a few dozen buildings when the fire spread, but the great thing is that almost everything there is made of cement and stucco, so it spread slowly. All the people are okay—well, besides those who died before we arrived. Better yet, they came out of their odd stupor a few weeks after they stopped eating the genetically modified food. Believe it or not, in the past month, the police had to arrest five people for being a public nuisance." She laughed.

I couldn't join her mirth. Not yet. "And Dona Mafalda's daughter?" I held my breath, seeing again the little children who'd stalked my dreams.

"Actually, Brigida's the reason we found you. Your tracking chip was damaged when you were burned, so at first we suspected the Emporium took you with them. But she reported to the police about you disappearing into a wheat field after saving them, and we had ears out waiting for just that kind of intel. We searched the field and found you. Burned to a crisp I might add. You must have been passed out there when the fire jumped to the field."

I might have also accidentally set it ablaze. "Her children?"

"They were a little hungry and a lot scared, but they're fine. Thanks to you. Often it's the wee ones who are the most resilient."

I let out a sigh, releasing the tension that had built inside me since waking. "That's good."

"The town will recover before too long, though the depressant will remain in their organs for years to come. However, only the pregnant women and their children are at immediate risk, and with the formulas I stole, we've managed to come up with some countermeasures to save the babies." A slight frown marred her face. "Some of the older people may still die before their time, but they're lucky we caught it when we did."

"At least it wasn't a virus that could spread like a biological weapon."

Kenna grimaced. "That's probably next on the Emporium's list." Her voice was light but deadly serious. "Regardless, we'll keep a sharp eye out for any more unexplained decreases in population. By the way, you were right. All the documentation points to their intention of eventually getting rid of any sick or aged who might be a drain on society. And they were pleased about the side effect of infant mortality because they felt it would help them control the mortal population."

"That control will never happen. Not while we're still alive."

Her hand slid into mine, sending a different kind of sensation pulsing through my body.

"You might have a fever," she said. "Your hand's burning."

"No, I . . ." How embarrassing to show my reaction to her this way. "Just a few overheated atoms."

"I like the sound of that." She leaned forward and kissed me. My hand went up around her neck pulling her close, enjoying the taste of her lips. She felt so good, and smelled even better. Far better than any drug.

I was about to investigate her mouth further when Ritter reentered the room, his hair still wet from his shower. "Feeling better, I see." His smile mocked, but his dark eyes danced with amusement.

Releasing Kenna reluctantly, I reached out and shook his hand. "Thank you for coming."

"How are you feeling?"

"Not great, but I think I'm going to be just fine."

"I knew you would be once you made the decision. I'm proud of you, son."

Ritter never gave praise unless it was merited, so this, and the way Kenna watched me with her baby blues, her lips moist and reddened with my kiss, finally made it all real. I had fought both the Emporium and my own personal dragon and had come up the victor.

"Is there anything I can do for you?" Ritter asked.

I started to shake my head and then remembered. "Well, there is this old guy I borrowed a motorcycle from. I really need to get him a replacement."

THE END

TEYLA BRANTON GREW UP AVIDLY READING SCIENCE FICTION and fantasy and watching Star Trek reruns with her large family. They lived on a little farm where she loved to visit the solitary cow and collect (and juggle) the eggs, usually making it back to the house with most of them intact. On that same farm she once owned thirty-three gerbils and eighteen cats, not a good mix, as it turns out. Teyla always had her nose in a book and daydreamed about someday creating her own worlds.

Teyla is now married, mostly grown up, and has seven kids, so life at her house can be very interesting (and loud), but writing keeps her sane. She thrives on the energy and daily amusement offered by her children, the semi-ordered chaos giving her a constant source of writing material. Grabbing any snatch of free time from her hectic life, Teyla writes novels, often with a child on her lap. She warns her children that if they don't behave, they just might find themselves in her next book! She's been known to wear pajamas all day when working on a deadline, and is often distracted enough to burn dinner. (Okay, pretty much 90% of the time.) A sign on her office door reads: DANGER. WRITER AT WORK. ENTER AT YOUR OWN RISK.

She loves writing fiction and traveling, and she hopes to write and travel a lot more. She also loves shooting guns, martial arts, and belly dancing. She has worked in the publishing business for over twenty years. Teyla also writes romance and suspense under the name Rachel Branton. For more information, please visit http://www.TeylaBranton.com.

www.ingramcontent.com/pod-product-compliance
Lightning Source LLC
Chambersburg PA
CBHW060942120626
46557CB00003B/1112